GHOST
Hunting

Ellis M. Reed

raintree
a Capstone company — publishers for children

Raintree is an imprint of Capstone Global Library Limited, a company incorporated in England and Wales having its registered office at 264 Banbury Road, Oxford, OX2 7DY – Registered company number: 6695582

www.raintree.co.uk
myorders@raintree.co.uk

Text © Capstone Global Library Limited 2019
The moral rights of the proprietor have been asserted.

All rights reserved. No part of this publication may be reproduced in any form or by any means (including photocopying or storing it in any medium by electronic means and whether or not transiently or incidentally to some other use of this publication) without the written permission of the copyright owner, except in accordance with the provisions of the Copyright, Designs and Patents Act 1988 or under the terms of a licence issued by the Copyright Licensing Agency, Barnard's Inn, 86 Fetter Lane, London, EC4A 1EN (www.cla.co.uk). Applications for the copyright owner's written permission should be addressed to the publisher.

Edited by Maddie Spalding
Designed by Becky Daum
Production by Colleen McLaren
Printed and bound in India

ISBN 978 1 4747 7364 5
22 21 20 19 18
10 9 8 7 6 5 4 3 2 1

Acknowledgments
AP Images: Bob Zellar/The Billings Gazette, 22–23, Greg Wahl-Stephens/Patron Spirits, 14–15; iStockphoto: cveltri, 20–21, inhauscreative, cover (foreground), jxfzsy, 26–27, RonTech2000, 8–9, suman bhaumik, 31; Shutterstock Images: Couperfield, 6–7, eddtoro, 12–13, Shutterstock, Evannovostro, cover (background), f11photo, 11, kryzhov, 5, Peter Kim, 24–25, RikoBest, 19, Zakrevsky Andrey, 16–17
Design Elements: iStockphoto, Red Line Editorial, and Shutterstock Images

Every effort has been made to contact copyright holders of material reproduced in this book. Any omissions will be rectified in subsequent printings if notice is given to the publisher.

All the internet addresses (URLs) given in this book were valid at the time of going to press. However, due to the dynamic nature of the internet, some addresses may have changed, or sites may have changed or ceased to exist since publication. While the author and publisher regret any inconvenience this may cause readers, no responsibility for any such changes can be accepted by either the author or the publisher.

CONTENTS

CHAPTER ONE
WHAT IS GHOST HUNTING? 4

CHAPTER TWO
GHOST HUNTING TEAMS 10

CHAPTER THREE
GHOST TECH 18

Glossary 28
Trivia 29
Activity 30
Find out more 32
Index 32

CHAPTER 1

WHAT IS GHOST hunting?

Have you ever seen a ghost? Maybe something grabbed your arm. Maybe you saw something move in an empty house. Maybe you heard a strange voice whisper in your ear! Was it the wind, or was it a ghost?

Ghost stories have been passed down for hundreds of years. Have you ever told a ghost story?

Some people try to talk to ghosts through a Ouija board. They spell out questions and hope a ghost will spell out its answers.

Ghost stories have been around for a long time. In the 1800s, a group of people wanted to prove ghosts were real.

Henry Sidgwick knew what to do. He started the Society for **Psychical** Research (SPR) in England. This group looked for **paranormal data**. They did many tests. They spoke to **mediums**. Mediums are people who say they can talk to ghosts.

THE SPR

The SPR is still around today. It helps people study **hauntings**.

GHOST HUNTERS

Some members of the SPR are ghost hunters. Ghost hunters look for ghosts. They search in scary places. They sometimes sleep in creepy hotels. They sometimes walk through **abandoned** hospitals.

Ghost hunters often try to talk to ghosts. Some people tell stories about unfriendly ghosts. They say these ghosts throw books or even scratch people. Ghost hunters try to make those ghosts leave.

Ghost hunters explore creepy places, such as old hotels, to find ghosts.

CHAPTER 2

GHOST HUNTING teams

Ghost hunting is popular. There are thousands of ghost hunting teams around the world. Some teams even have television shows.

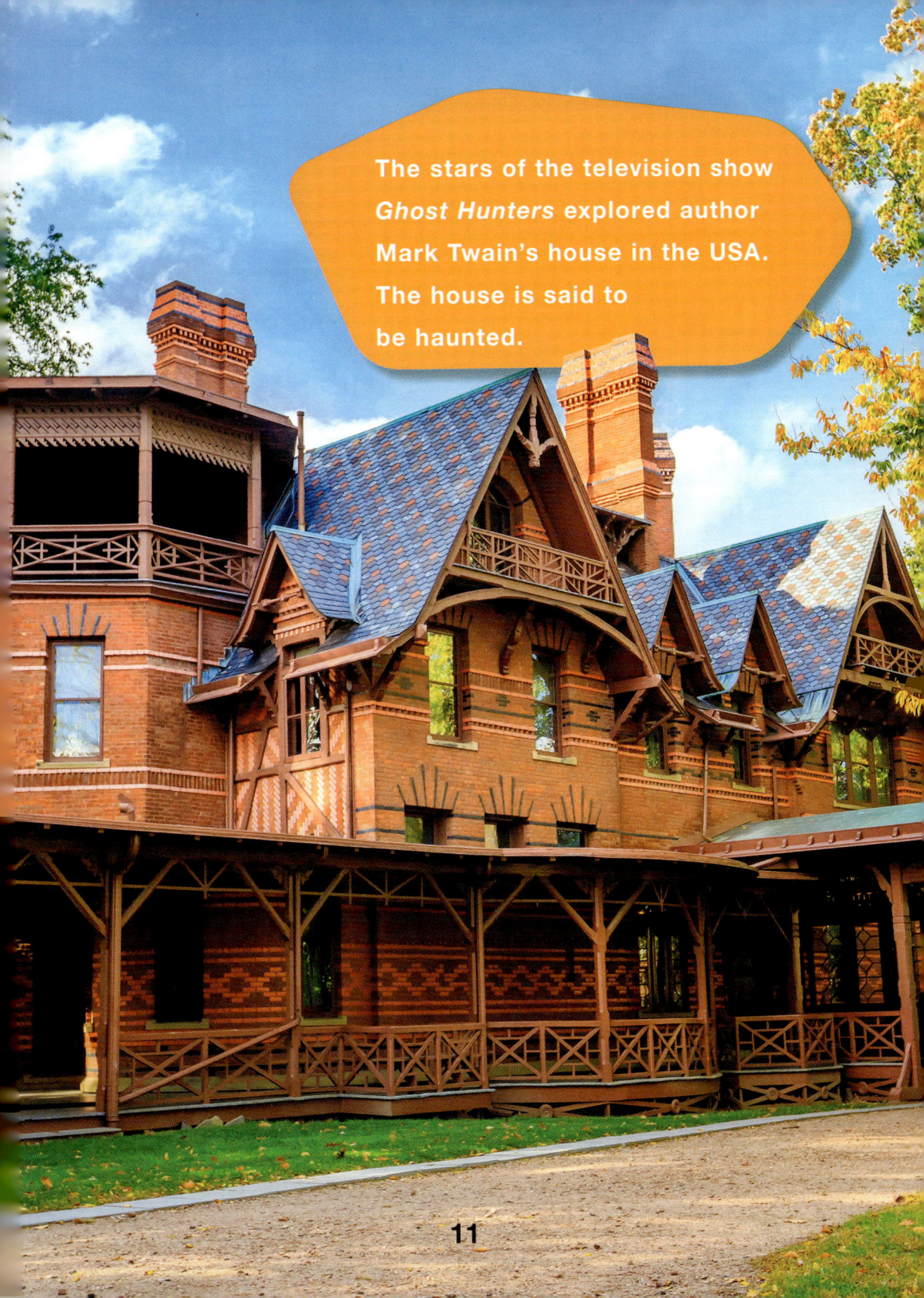

The stars of the television show *Ghost Hunters* explored author Mark Twain's house in the USA. The house is said to be haunted.

PART OF A TEAM

Ghost hunters like to work in teams. Ghost hunting can be unsafe. It is good to hunt with other people. Someone can then help you if you get hurt.

FUNNY GHOST HUNTERS

There are ghost hunting shows on YouTube. *BuzzFeed Unsolved* looks for proof of ghosts, aliens and monsters.

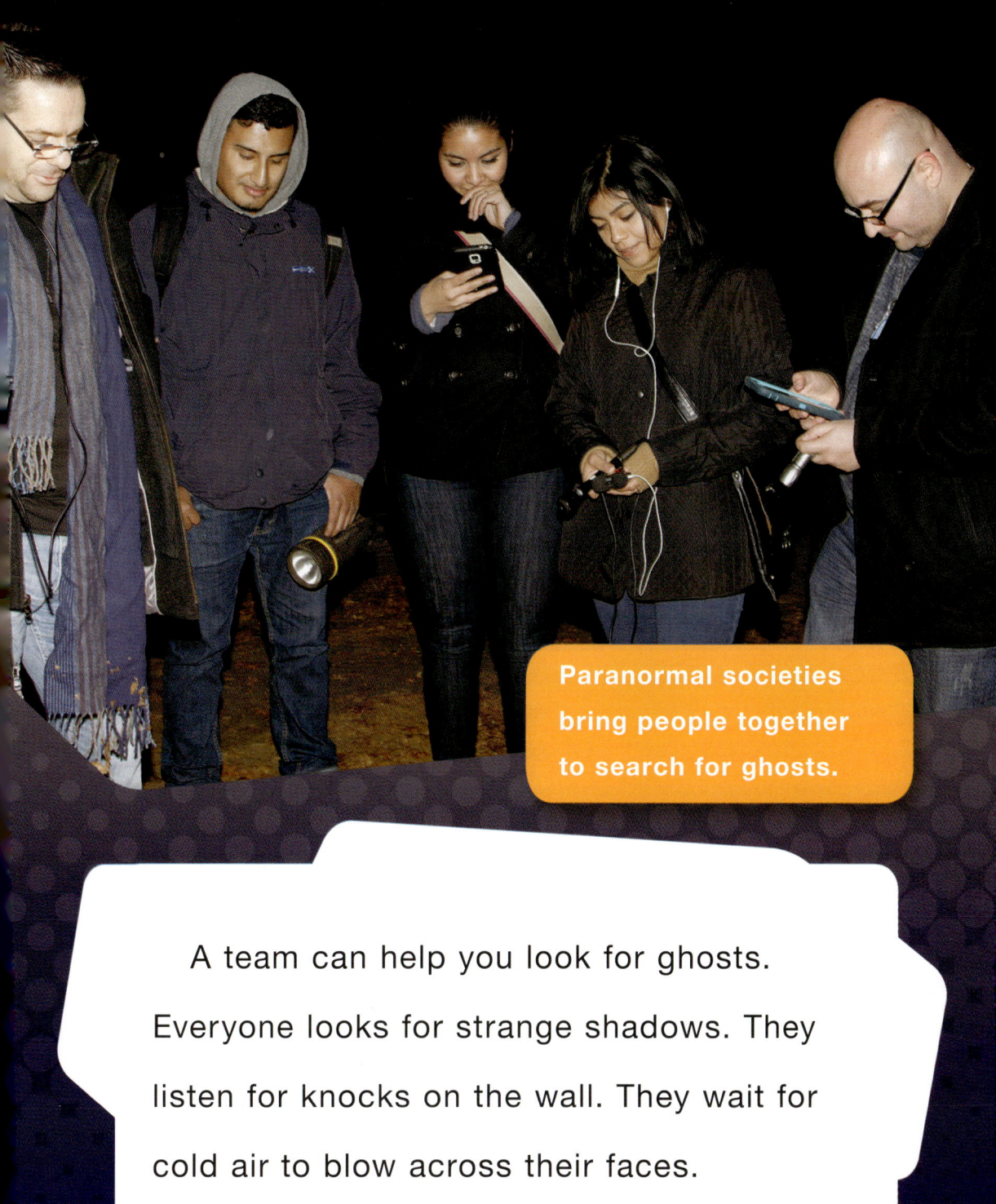

Paranormal societies bring people together to search for ghosts.

A team can help you look for ghosts. Everyone looks for strange shadows. They listen for knocks on the wall. They wait for cold air to blow across their faces.

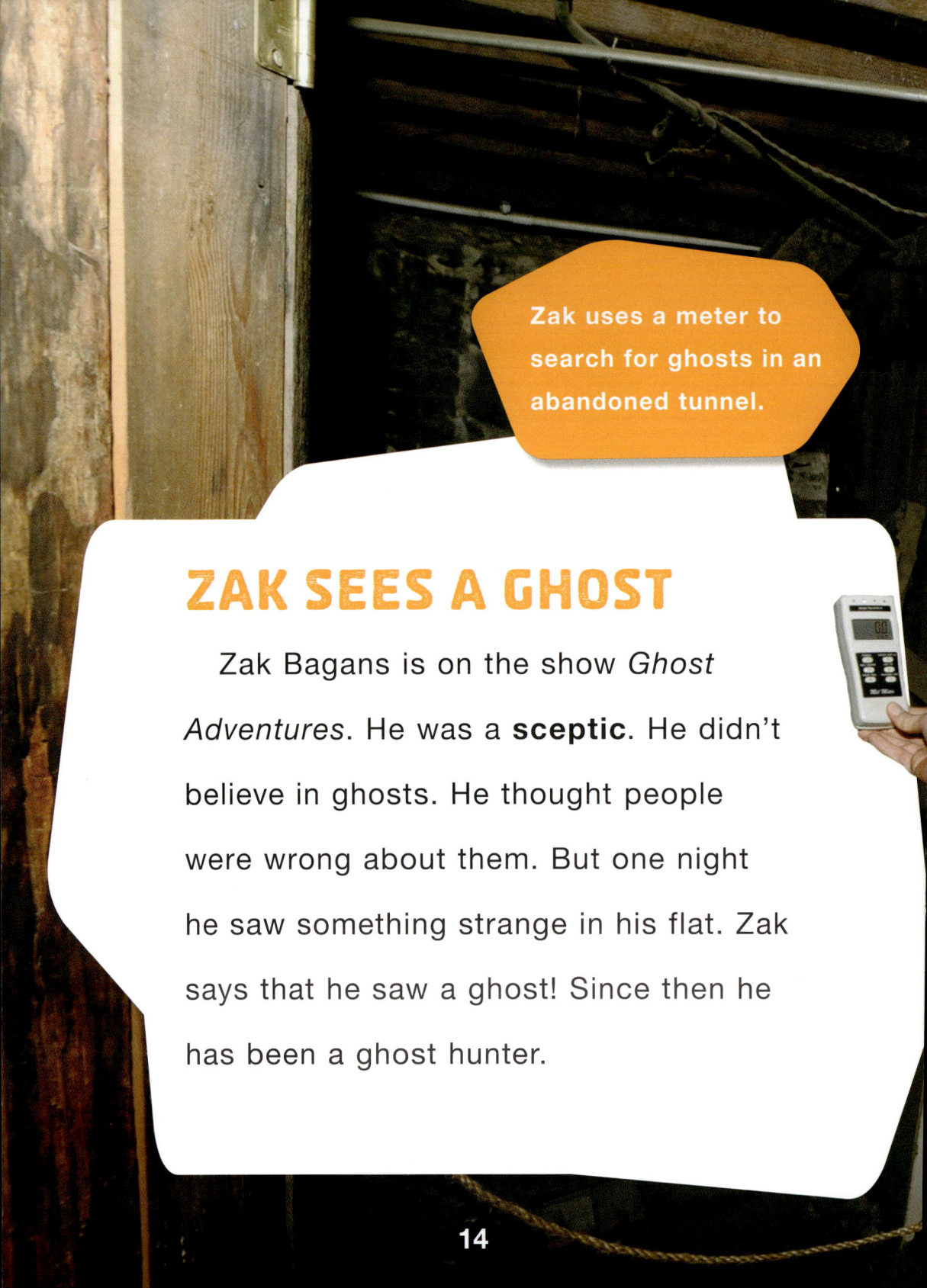

Zak uses a meter to search for ghosts in an abandoned tunnel.

ZAK SEES A GHOST

Zak Bagans is on the show *Ghost Adventures*. He was a **sceptic**. He didn't believe in ghosts. He thought people were wrong about them. But one night he saw something strange in his flat. Zak says that he saw a ghost! Since then he has been a ghost hunter.

Some abandoned islands are said to be haunted.

Zak and his team hunt together. They go to many places. They see strange things. But one thing really scared Zak.

Zak's team went to an island in Italy. Many people died there long ago. Zak started to feel bad inside a room. He then got very angry. He yelled at his teammate Aaron. He wanted to fight Aaron. Zak's team helped him outside. Soon Zak started to feel better. He thinks he was **possessed** by a spirit.

CHAPTER 3

GHOST tech

Everyone on a ghost hunting team is looking for ghosts. But they all have different jobs to do. Electronic devices help them.

CAMERAS

Ghost hunters have many cameras. Some show heat. They are **thermal** cameras. Hot things show up as red. Cold things are blue. These cameras help ghost hunters see in the dark.

Thermal cameras show how much or how little heat something gives off.

The team on *Ghost Adventures* uses an Xbox Kinect. It is a video game system. It uses a camera. The Kinect can show the shape of a person on the screen. It sometimes shows shapes in an empty room. One time, a shape looked like it was waving hello!

Ghost hunters use radios to listen for ghosts.

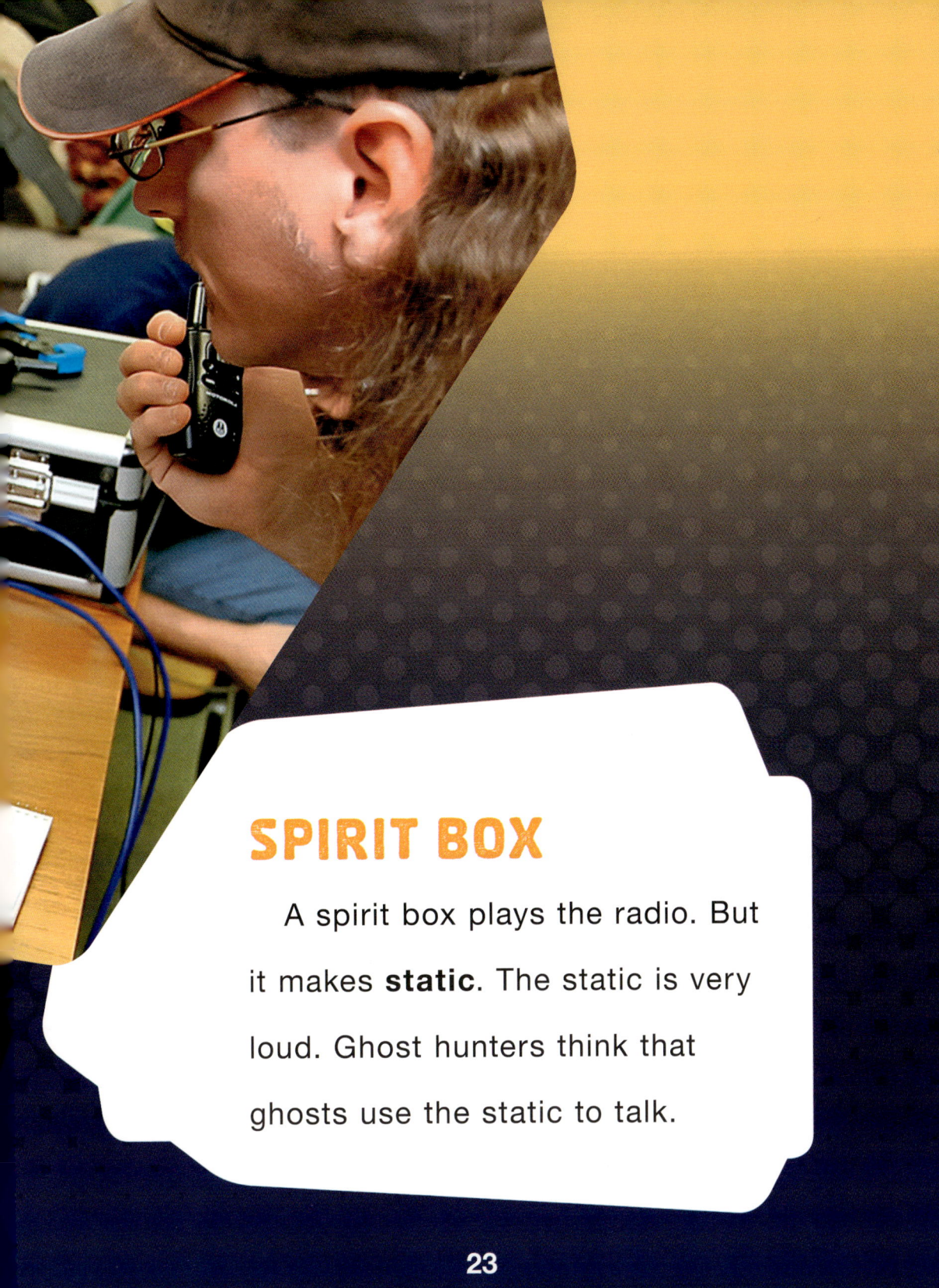

SPIRIT BOX

A spirit box plays the radio. But it makes **static**. The static is very loud. Ghost hunters think that ghosts use the static to talk.

There's sometimes a noise in the static. It can sound like words. It might be an answer to a question. Ghost hunters listen carefully. They have to pay attention. They don't want to miss the message. Some hunters have heard words such as "spirit" and "help". They have even heard their names.

QUESTIONING A GHOST

Teams may ask a ghost's name. They may ask the ghost how it died. What questions would you ask a ghost?

Some EMF meters have needles. The needle moves to higher numbers when there's a spike in energy.

ENERGY METER

Do ghosts give off energy? Ghost hunters think so. An electromagnetic field (EMF) meter finds changes in energy. The meter fits in your hand. Some meters have coloured lights. The colour changes when there's a **spike** in energy. This change might mean a ghost is nearby.

Ghost hunters use many types of equipment. This equipment gives them data. This data might help prove that they found a ghost.

GLOSSARY

abandoned
no longer used

data
facts that are collected

haunting
a mysterious event, possibly caused by a visit from a ghost

medium
a person who is said to be able to talk to ghosts

paranormal
something spooky that can't be explained with science, such as ghosts

possessed
to be taken over and controlled by something else

psychical
relating to ghosts or spirits

sceptic
a person who doesn't believe in something that others do

spike
a sudden rise

static
background noise created by televisions and radios

thermal
having to do with temperature

TRIVIA

1. Thirty-four per cent of people in Britain believe in ghosts. Nine per cent say they have spoken to a ghost.

2. EMF meters find changes in the energy around us. But there is no proof that ghosts give off this energy. EMF meters can even pick up extra energy from mobile phones.

3. Ghost hunting can be dangerous. In 2010, some ghost hunters wanted to see a ghost train in North Carolina, USA. Twelve people stood on the train tracks. But a real train was coming. The people had to run very fast to get out of the way. One person was killed.

ACTIVITY

Do you think there is a ghost in your house? You can become a ghost hunter to find out! Form a team with friends who want to be ghost hunters too.

Most mobile phones have video cameras. Put one in a room of your house. Turn on the camera. You can start asking questions. You might ask, "Is there anyone else in the room right now?" You could say, "If you are here right now, show me!" Write down anything strange that happens.

You can watch the video later with your team. Maybe there's a scary noise that you didn't hear at the time. Maybe you see a strange light in the video. Think about what might cause these things. Was there an animal in the next room? Was the light from an open window? If not, it may have been a ghost!

FIND OUT MORE

Books
Ghosts in Hotels, Lisa Owings (Bellwether Media, 2017)

The Voice in the Boys' Room (Michael Dahl's Really Scary Stories), Michael Dahl (Stone Arch Books, 2016)

True Stories of Ghosts, Paul Dowswell (Usborne, 2012)

Websites
A 'haunted Britain' interactive map
www.visitbritain.com/gb/en/haunted-britain-explore-our-map

An introduction to ghost investigating
kids.ghostvillage.com/jrghosthunters/index.shtml

The History Channel's history of ghost stories
www.history.com/topics/halloween/historical-ghost-stories

INDEX

Bagans, Zak 14, 16–17
BuzzFeed Unsolved 12
electromagnetic field (EMF) meter 27

Ghost Adventures 14, 20
ghost hunters 8, 10, 12–14, 16–17
ghost stories 6, 8
mediums 7

Sidgwick, Henry 7
Society for Psychical Research (SPR) 7–8
spirit box 23–24
thermal cameras 19
Xbox Kinect 20